D0537173

©2001 Bookmart Limited

All rights reserved. No part of this publication may be reproduced stored in a retrieval system or transmitted by any means, electronic, mechanical, photocopying or otherwise, without the prior permission of the publisher.

Published by
Armadillo Books
an imprint of
Bookmart Limited
Registered Number 2372865
Trading as Bookmart Limited
Desford Road
Enderby
Leicester LE9 5AD

ISBN 1-84322-003-2

Produced for
Bookmart Limited by
Nicola Baxter
PO Box 215,
Framingham Earl
Norwich NR14 7UR

Designer: Amanda Hawkes
Production designer: Amy Barton

Printed in China

Starting to read – no trouble!

This story of tropical trouble helps to make sharing books at home successful and enjoyable. The book can be used in several ways to help beginning readers gain confidence.

You could start by reading the illustrated words at the edge of each lefthand page with your child. Have fun trying to spot the same words in the story itself.

All the words on the righthand pages have already been met on the facing page. Help your child to read these by pointing out words and groups of words already met.

Finally, all the illustrated words can be found at the end of the book. Enjoy checking all the words you can both read!

With lots of
hugs & kisses.
aunty
to
March 2002

Trouble
in the
Jungle

Written by Nicola Baxter · Illustrated by Geoff Ball

ARMADILLO

jungle

Alan

Jack

rucksack

One day, two friends called Alan and Jack set off into the jungle.

"Why do I have to carry everything?" asks Jack.

His rucksack is very heavy.

Alan does not hear a thing. He is hurrying ahead.

Alan is not carrying a thing!

trees

leaf

face

gorilla

Alan pushes on through the trees.

Thwack! A big leaf smacks Jack in the face ... hard.

"Ow!" cries Jack. "Be careful, Alan! That hurts!"

But Alan does not hear. He is being hugged ... by a gorilla!

"Ow!" cries Alan. "That hurts, gorilla!"

sandwich

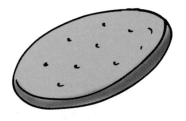

biscuit

apple

banana

The gorilla will not let go!

"Give him something to eat!" cries Alan at last.

Jack opens his rucksack.

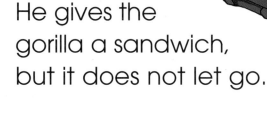

He gives the gorilla a sandwich, but it does not let go.

He gives the gorilla a biscuit and an apple, but it does not let go.

He gives the gorilla a banana.

The gorilla lets go at last!

stick

hat

crisps

grapes

Alan picks up a big stick to shake at any gorillas! He hurries on again.

Suddenly, a parrot hops on to his hat!

"Help!" cries Alan.

"Go away!" says Jack to the parrot, but it does not fly away.

Jack gives the parrot some crisps, but it does not fly away.

He gives it some grapes.

"Go away!" says the parrot!

photo

monkey

branch

camera

"I feel silly," says Alan, "with a parrot on my head!"

"You look silly!" says the parrot.

Jack laughs.

"I must take a photo of you!" he says.

Oh no! A monkey is sitting on a branch. He snatches the camera!

The monkey takes a photo of Alan!

binoculars

snake

bush

path

"Give me the binoculars!" says Alan. "I won't let a monkey take **them**."

Suddenly, a snake slithers on to Jack's rucksack.

"Help!" cries Jack! "Snakes bite!"

But the snake is comfortable. It does not move.

Jack pulls off his rucksack. He leaves it under a bush beside the path.

"I won't let a snake bite me!" he says.

birds

animals

feathers

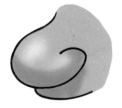

nose

"The jungle is full of cheeky birds and animals," says Alan.

Now the parrot's feathers are tickling his nose.

"Atishoo!" says Alan.

"Bless you," says the parrot.

Jack hurries ahead.

"Wait for me!" calls Alan. He is carrying a stick, the binoculars and the parrot!

Jack does not slow down.

He is not carrying anything now!

Picture dictionary

Now you can read these words!

Alan

animals

apple

banana

binoculars

birds

biscuit

branch

bush

camera

crisps

face

feathers

gorilla

grapes

hat

Jack

leaf

monkey

nose

path

photo

rucksack

sandwich

snake

stick

trees